Rotary

Club of Benton Harbor
Sunrise

This book is a gift to you and your family
from the Benton Harbor Sunrise Rotary
Club.
Happy Reading!!

This book
belongs to

_____

All rights reserved. Published by Spectacled Bear Publishing.

For information, address Spectacled Bear Publishing, 2929 Villa Lane, Benton Harbor, MI 49022.

Printed in Marceline, MO
First Edition

LCCN 2016906585, ISBN: 978-0-9975099-0-8 (hard cover)

by Anne Brandt
pictures by Annie Poon

Philip & Phoebe

for
Kevin & Keith

This is Philip.
He wears a red cape just like a superhero.

This is Phoebe, his baby sister.
She loves giraffes.

Whenever she cried, everyone ran to see what was wrong.

And whenever she laughed, everyone ran to see what she was happy about.

Whenever Philip cried, someone said,
"There, there, big boys don't cry."

And whenever he laughed, someone said, "My, but you are childish!"

Philip felt
left out.

One starry night Philip had an idea.
"Maybe if I wish very hard I can change
Phoebe into something else."

He climbed
out of bed and
tiptoed into
her room.

Phoebe wasn't
laughing or
crying. She
was sleeping.

Philip looked at Phoebe. He closed his eyes and clenched his fists.

He thought, "I wish, I wish, I wish Phoebe was a horse." There wasn't a sound.

Suddenly...

There before him on the floor stood the most beautiful horse he had ever seen.

He climbed into the red saddle as Phoebe's tail swished from side to side.

But Phoebe had a mind of her own.
She galloped and galloped.
She galloped so fast Philip
had no time to breathe.
Faster and faster,
up over the
furniture they
went.

He shut his eyes and said,
"I wish, I wish, I wish Phoebe
was an ice cream cone."

Philip felt the black horse disappear beneath him. Instead he found himself sitting on the nursery room rug in his pajamas... with an ice cream cone in his hand!

It was his favorite flavors too: Chocolate, coconut, and marshmallow.

Philip raised the cone to his mouth for the first lick. It was delicious! He took a second lick. It was just as good as the first.
And so was the third.

And the fourth.

And the fifth.

But Philip noticed there was just as much ice cream as there was in the beginning.

"Oh, dear, what will I do with the rest of Phoebe?

Maybe I'll wish for something else."

grrrrowl

"I wish Phoebe was a big fire engine." Then Philip saw it. The fire truck Phoebe.

But what a shock!

Phoebe was a broken down, rickety fire truck with flat tires and a very cracked window. One of her ladders was missing too.

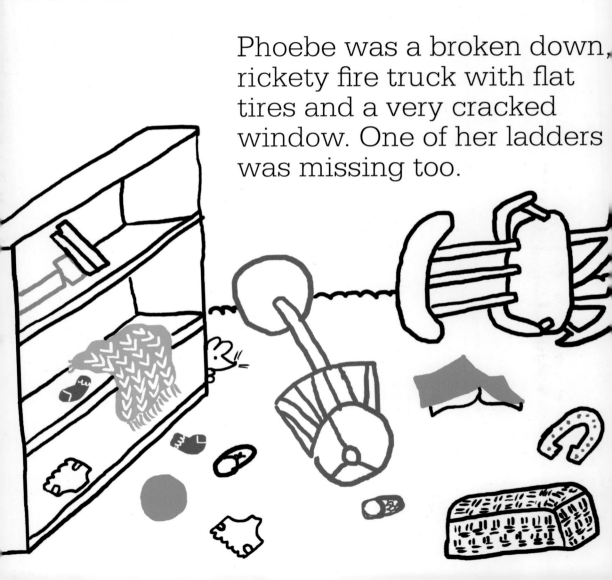

She hardly budged when Philip
pushed her around the floor.

Philip was unhappy.

He said in his unhappiest voice,
"You aren't much fun as a sister,
but you aren't fun as a horse or an
ice cream cone or a fire truck either."

Then he said, "I wish, I wish, I wish you were my little sister." Boy, he never thought he'd be wishing that! The next time Philip looked in the crib, there was the real Phoebe.

And she was sound asleep.

Anne Brandt, writer, has loved words forever. She was a freelance writer for twenty-five years and still found time to create and promote her own work. Anne has written children's stories, short fiction, plays, poems, novels, and a collection of personal essays titled *The Square Root of Someone*. In addition, she has been an active blogger since 2004 and recently won several honors for her flash fiction. She also plays "at" the piano. Visit Anne at annebrandt.com

Annie Poon, illustrator, learned to draw as a child by copying characters off cereal boxes and comic books. Today she has a BFA in drawing and painting from Manhattan's School of Visual Arts. Annie loves to create stop-motion animations from cut paper, and her animation "Runaway Bathtub" is among the MoMA's collections. Much of her work revolves around animals, and her most recent book is *Oh Puppy!* For *Philip and Phoebe*, she was inspired by several monochromatic illustrators as well as her niece and a young boy she knows. Annie also likes to write music. Visit Annie at anniepoon.com

Keith Carollo, graphic designer, got to work on this book with his two best friends. He is writing and designing a book project of his own and it is sort of about rainbows. Visit Keith at keithcarollo.com

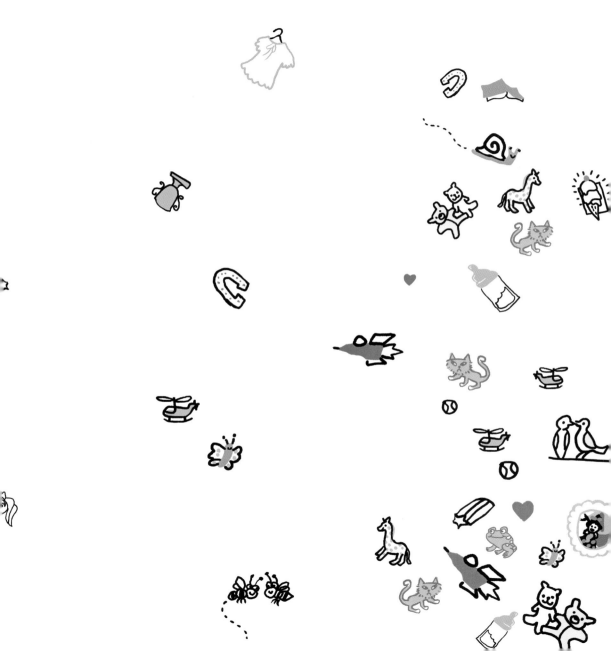

Can you find these items in the story of Philip & Phoebe?